A Day At The Old Man's Garden

AND FULTON STREET.

By

W. K. Willowbough

W. G. KASEBERG PUBLISHING

GLEN CARBON, ILLINOIS

A DAY AT THE OLD MAN'S GARDEN
by W. K. Willowbough

First Edition, First Printing
Published by
W. G. Kaseberg Publishing
49 Red Bud Lane, Glen Carbon, Illinois 62034

Cover and book design, typography & composition by
Arrow Graphics, Inc.
Watertown, Massachusetts
info@arrow1.com
Printed in China

ISBN: 0-9761138-0-5
Library of Congress Control Number:
2004113483

A Legacy

The following true narratives are passed on in the tradition of "Uncle Bill" (1876–1965). The kindest and gentlest of men, he often captivated us children with wonderful stories about his own outdoor experiences, each one invariably providing an enlightening glimpse into the quite remarkable intelligence and character of our small indigenous wildlife neighbors.

For Joan

Countless are the things thou hast made,
O Lord. Thou hast made all by thy wisdom;
and the earth is full of thy creatures, beasts
both great and small.

Psalm 104: 24.

t was a dark and stormy night, but now, all the thunder and lightning, strong winds and cold drenching rain have passed by. It's the first week of June and a new day is beginning in a small town in southern Illinois. Wispy white clouds scattered overhead in the bright blue morning sky and a cool clean-smelling breeze coming out of the west promise a beautiful spring day.

As the sun breaks free from the horizon, two cottontail rabbits are grazing on the lawn behind a small brown house at the end of a quiet suburban cul-de-sac. The rabbits are Old Mrs. Bun and one of her daughters, Little-Bitty Bun.

Old Mrs. Bun, about nine years old and quite elderly by rabbit standards, is a mother and a grandmother many times over. Her arched muzzle, grizzled coat and bare, dark-skinned, ragged tips of her ears show her age, but she's a cool, street-savvy old gal who still can outrun and outsmart any dog around.

Little-Bitty Bun is one of the very few of last year's baby rabbits to have survived the first full year of life. Through last summer, and over the long cold winter, she grew up, matured and learned many lessons about surviving in a rabbit's dangerous world. Now, as a young doe, she's learning how to be a good mother.

While they appear to leisurely munch on the crisp wet grass, clover and dandelions in the yard, both rabbits keep their eyes and ears alert for any danger that might appear and, as well, for any sound or sign indicating that the old man who lives in the small brown house soon might be coming outside.

From the wet tree branches overhead, birds and squirrels are also keeping an eye on the house. And two chipmunks, one huddled beneath a deck chair on the house's back porch and using her furry tail as a foot warmer, and the other sitting atop a pile of firewood stacked just off the porch, are watching and listening, as well.

Like the rabbits, the two chipmunks are related. The chipmunk on the woodpile is Itchy Bob, a brash, impetuous three year-old male who sports only half a tail. He lost the other half last summer, in a narrow escape from a neighborhood cat.

Before that, he was just called Itchy, because he always seems to be "just itchin'" for adventure of one kind or another. Even having his tail bobbed by a cat hasn't persuaded him to reform his ways.

Beneath the deck chair is Itchy Bob's sister, Shelley. She's practical, polite and an exceptionally gentle and devoted mother. But, as proper and gracious as she is, if pushed too far, she can hip check like a tough hockey player. She also holds the neighborhood record for stowing the most peanuts into her cheeks: five double-nutters. It's a practical talent for a chipmunk to have, but not a very pretty thing to see.

From the woodpile, Itchy Bob keeps one eye on the house's big glass back door and the other on the mischievous squirrels in the tree above him. Below, Shelley just concentrates on the back door.

Many of the birds and animals gathered here are grooming themselves while they wait, trying to dry out and freshen up rain-soaked feathers or fur in the brisk morning air. A gray squirrel half-way up the small fan-shaped mulberry tree located just off the porch and opposite the back door, is using her paws to brush and fluff up her long fleecy tail. In the large birdbath below the tree, a bright red male cardinal vigorously splashes away. Every few moments, he pauses to glance over at the back door, then resumes his bath.

These birds and small animals know that they're welcome in this yard. Some make homes and raise their families here. Others live in neighboring yards, meadows or woods and come to visit almost every day. They've all come to know the old man who lives here and to recognize him by sight and the sound of his voice. Likewise, the old man, through patience and attention, has learned many of their calls, habits and personalities. Sometimes, they all seem to understand one another — and more often than you might think, they do.

The rabbits, chipmunks and a few of the birds are best friends of the old man. They've known and trusted him for years, many of them, since they were babies. Most of the other birds and animals are good neighbors, but a few, like the squirrels and blue jays, just can't seem to help being mischievous scamps. But to all of them, best friends, good neighbors and scamps alike, this yard is a very special place where they know they are cared about. This is the old man's garden.

All of them look expectantly to thee to give them their food at the proper time; what thou givest them they gather up, when thou openest thy hand, they eat their fill.

Psalm 104: 27-28.

hen it happens. The blinds behind the big glass back door slowly draw back and there, looking out at them, is the old man. He tap-tap-taps on the glass with his finger and smiles broadly at his friends as he pulls on his old wide-brimmed hat and steps into his big garden boots. The chipmunks quickly scamper up to the door to peer in as the old man fills his coat pockets with peanuts and raisin oatmeal cookies. Impatiently, Itchy Bob stands up on his hind legs and presses his nose against the glass while using his front paws to shade his eyes from the pane's reflected glare.

Down the mulberry tree come three squirrels, loudly grousing and flicking their tails in displeasure over the chipmunks having beat them to the head of the line. Avoiding the rowdy squirrels, the cardinal stops his bath and flies up into the tall ash tree in the middle of the yard. But before the squirrels can become too quarrelsome, the door opens and the old man spryly steps out onto the porch.

"Hey guys," he calls out, happily. "Did everybody keep warm and dry last night? That's the ticket!"

A robust male robin swoops down from the eaves of the porch where he and his mate have their nest, and chirps loudly as he alights on the rim of the birdbath beneath the mulberry tree.

"There's that ol' fat robin!" announces the old man cheerfully. "How's it goin' Fatty? You gettin' after those ol' bugs and worms, already? That's the stuff!"

When Fatty bends forward for a sip of water, the old man notices that, for the third day now, one of the long brown feathers on his lower back is askew, sticking up in the air and twisted like a stubborn cowlick. "Haven't got that silly ol' thing fixed yet, huh Fatty?" observes the old man.

Fatty gives an annoyed backward glance at the uncooperative feather, takes another sip of water, then glides low across the yard out toward the big vegetable garden. Landing on the run, he takes several quick steps and hops to a stop. Suddenly, Fatty cocks his head sharply downward to the left and freezes. With a little bounce, he pivots his whole body to the left and stabs his beak down hard at the ground, nabbing a big brown beetle.

"There you go, Fatty!" the old man calls out from the porch. "Yessiree, that 'ol robin's business is bugs and he means business."

Feeling a presence on the toe of his boot, the old man looks down to see Itchy Bob boldly perched there and staring up at him expectantly. Shelley, more reserved than her impatient brother, waits politely on the porch behind him, sitting up with her front paws resting across her chest.

"Chip-monkeys?" exclaims the old man loudly, pretending to be surprised. "Hey, Itchy Bob. Mornin', Shelley. You're both lookin' bright-eyed and bushy-tailed this mornin'.

Itchy Bob gives the old man a somewhat annoyed stare.

"Hey, sorry Bob — no offense. You know I think your tail's real… well, uh, distinguished lookin' — sorta like a Mohawk — sure, you know, spunky."

Apology accepted, Itchy Bob climbs over the old man's boot and reaches up with both front paws to the cuff of his trousers.

"What?" asks the old man. "Peanuts? Sure, we can do that."

Stooping, the old man holds out his palm filled with peanuts. While Itchy Bob picks over the pile, Shelley politely takes the peanut nearest her and starts shredding the shell to get at the roasted treat inside. Smiling at Shelley, the old man says, "There's a good girl. That's one little chip-monkey who hasn't forgot her Emily Post."

The chipmunks become nervous when three impatient squirrels begin prowling back and forth behind them on the porch. "Okay, all you fuzzytails, cool it," the old man tells the squirrels as he tosses a peanut toward each of them with his other hand.

As the squirrels scramble after their peanuts in a frenzy, a blue jay swoops down and tries to steal one as it bounces crazily across the porch's concrete surface. But the jay's not quick enough. A squirrel pounces on the peanut, picks it up between its nose and front paws, sniffs it, and satisfied with the aroma, nimbly scampers back up the mulberry tree.

Frustrated, the jay looks back at the old man and, bobbing his head up and down, pipes mournfully, "Wheedle, wheedle, wheedle."

"Aced out by a squirrel, huh?" notes the old man. "Boy, Jasper, you're slippin'. Okay, here's one just for you," he says as he tosses a peanut to the jay. "Now, promise t'be a good boy today."

Making three quick sideways hops to the peanut, the jay snatches it up in his beak and, pausing to cast a greedy glance back at the peanuts in the old man's palm, turns and flies away.

The jay flies over the little seasonal stream that runs along the west side of the old man's yard, across the meadow just beyond and into a small woods. As he watches the jay fly off, the old man notices that the stream is running fast and almost full from last night's rainstorm.

Looking back down at the two chipmunks, the old man asks, "All loaded up, you guys?"

Itchy Bob, with cheeks bulging and a big double-nutter sticking out of the front of his mouth like a very large cigar, glances up at the old man, then turns and sprints away, south, his jaunty half-tail pointed straight up in the air.

"Watch out for that cat," the old man calls out after him, chuckling. "You haven't got much tail left to spare."

Itchy Bob bounds along the flagstone path through the gravel that surrounds the porch, down to the lawn. At the lawn, he turns left and dashes along the top of the low stone wall that separates gravel from grass as it curves back beneath the branches of the tall old fir tree that stands at the southwest corner of the house.

At the end of the wall, Itchy Bob jumps up onto a low branch of the fir tree, close to the trunk, and freezes. From this higher vantage point he looks and listens for any sign of trouble ahead, around the corner of the house. Then, sure that his route is clear, he takes off lickety-split, toward the front of the house and his burrow deep beneath the old man's driveway.

"How're you doin', Shelley, 'bout set?" asks the old man.

Having eaten one peanut, Shelley's loaded up her cheeks with more to take home to her family. After some adjustments to her load, she starts out for her burrow but stops short when the old man asks, "What? No spitter?"

As Shelley begins redistributing the load between her cheeks to make room for a spitter, the old man sorts through the peanuts in his hand. Choosing a big triple-nutter, the old man holds it out towards her. "Now, here's a dandy spitter, but it's a biggie. Can you get it?" he asks, cautiously.

Shelley runs back to the old man and, standing up on her hind legs, inspects the big triple-nutter. After one more adjustment to her load, Shelley takes the spitter and, holding it between her front paws like a harmonica, pushes her mouth hard against its middle, straining to get a grip on it with her teeth. Finally, she bites into the shell and, with the giant peanut held crosswise in her teeth, the way a pirate might carry his cutlass when boarding an enemy ship, she races away, north, headed for her burrow in a neighbor's yard, around the end of the cul-de-sac from the old man's house.

While running along the west edge of the thick ground cover of violets and periwinkle that fills the yard on the north side of the old man's house, Shelley is ambushed by a squirrel who rushes at her headlong down the trunk of a tall red oak tree. She immediately spits out the triple-nutter into the grass to her left and dives to her right, deep into the ground cover. Just as she hoped, the squirrel goes after the spitter instead of her.

After a few moments of weaving her way through the tangle of periwinkle and violets, Shelley's bounding away, up the stair-stepped flagstone path that leads from the back yard, through the ground cover, up to the front yard. Upon reaching the front lawn, she stops and stands erect on her hind legs to look back. Seeing that the squirrel is back up the oak tree, clinging upside down along the side of the trunk with the triple-nutter in its mouth, Shelley knows she's put that problem far behind her.

With her tail bushed out and straight up in the air, Shelley dashes across an area of open lawn at warp speed, sprinting along in low rapid bounds like a flat stone skipping across the smooth surface of a pond. She leaps up at the trunk of a large black locust tree and pushes off hard, making a sharp left turn toward some shrubbery at the front of the old man's neighbor's house. She's halfway home now and, in the protection of the bushes, she pauses for a moment to catch her breath.

Meanwhile, in the back yard, it's the rabbits' turn for treats. From his porch, the old man looks out toward the wild flower garden that lies beside the little stream at the edge of his yard and calls out, "Any cookie customers, this mornin'? Any dandy little bunnies out here thinkin' about that ol' breakfast cookie and all those sweet, soft, chewy raisins?"

Looking over at Old Mrs. Bun, he grins, "There's that Ol' Bun — now, I know she's a cookie girl."

Old Mrs. Bun, chewing, looks up from a thick stand of clover, then takes two hops to her right, stopping at a very tall just-bloomed dandelion. She gives the bright yellow bud a deep pleasing sniff, then runs her nose quickly down the long smooth stem, through the grass all the way to the ground, and bites it off. Sitting back, she slowly munches on the crisp, crunchy, hollow dandelion stalk, starting at the bottom end.

In much the same way that a little kid eats a long piece of spaghetti, she draws the stalk further into her mouth with each bite, and soon, little by little, the whole long stem disappears. For just a moment, with only the flower still visible, Old Mrs. Bun looks as if she's sucking on a large, frilly, bright yellow pacifier. Then, in one big quick gulp, "thwo-o-o-p," she draws the whole dandelion flower into her mouth.

Looking very much contented as she savors the last and tastiest part of the dandelion, Old Mrs. Bun doesn't seem to notice the old man at all. But, of course, she does. She's just playing a little game with him — a game that they both enjoy — a game they play almost every morning.

The old man steps off the porch, walks across the gravel and slowly sits down on the low stone wall at the edge of the lawn. He leans far forward, smiling wide, and proudly declares, "That Ol' Bun's my buddy, she's such a good girl."

Old Mrs. Bun just gazes down at the ground through half-closed eyes, still slowly chewing up the last of the dandelion flower and now mixing in a small nibble of clover.

Then the old man says the magic words. Tilting his head down and rolling his eyes upward to their corners, he shyly peeks up at her with a low sidelong glance and, as if honey were dripping from his tongue, affectionately coos, "She's just an ol' sweetie pie."

Old Mrs. Bun's ears perk straight up and she immediately turns toward the old man. She fixes her gaze on him, opens her eyes very, very wide as if to say, "Oh, there you are!" and quickly hops directly over to him.

"Sure, that ol' Bun's a cookie girl," declares the old man as Old Mrs. Bun stares up anxiously at him, twitching her nose.

"Ooooh, lotsa raisins in this ol' cookie, Bun," he says as he breaks a cookie and holds out half of it to her. "Just look at all those sweet, soft, chewy raisins."

Old Mrs. Bun slowly stretches forward, looking up into the old man's smiling face all the while. She sniffs the back of his hand then tenderly presses her velvety soft nose against it. Very daintily, she takes the cookie in her mouth and, turning, hops a short distance away, along the base of the low stone wall to a favorite spot beneath the low fragrant branches of the big fir tree.

Having waited as long as politeness could possibly require for her mother to be served first, Little-Bitty Bun now quickly hops right up to the old man's boots.

"Well, here's another cookie customer," exclaims the old man, happily. "That Little-Bitty Bun's just all grown up into such a pretty young lady. She gets after that ol' cookie — sure, she does. That Little-Bitty Bun's a cookie girl."

As she sits up tall to receive her cookie, the old man notices that Little-Bitty Bun's belly looks pinkish and has less fur than it normally does. That means that she has new babies, because when a mother rabbit gives birth, she digs a small burrow and lines it with soft dry grass and bits of warm fur that she plucks from her belly with her teeth. Certain that now she'll be hungrier than usual, the old man breaks off an extra-big piece of cookie for her.

"Oh boy, just look at all the raisins in that ol' cookie," says the old man as he holds it out to Little-Bitty Bun.

Eagerly, but politely, she takes the cookie from his hand, hops a short distance out into the lawn and crouches down in the grass to enjoy her breakfast treat.

While checking his pockets' supply of treats, the old man notices some movement in the big shady perennial flower bed that lies along the edge of the porch, just below the little fan-shaped mulberry tree. Turning right in his seat on the stone wall, he spots a new little friend slowly making her way out from beneath the broad sprawling leaves and big white lacy flowers of a patch of bishop's weed.

"Well, who's this funny little sleepyhead just wakin' up?" he teases playfully.

Born early this spring in a burrow in the thick ground cover along the north side of the old man's house, Bittiest Bun is just a tiny little girl, about one fourth the size of her mother, Little-Bitty Bun. She has been on her own for about a month, exploring around the yard, locating good hiding places and finding out which plants are good to eat. A week ago, she learned that the old man's raisin oatmeal cookies were simply irresistible and she has been showing up for breakfast and bedtime cookies ever since.

"That Bittiest Bun's a dandy little bunny — a big-D dandy," brags the old man, busting his buttons. "She's just gettin' s-o-o big! She's just gettin' bigger every day!"

As small as she is, Bittiest Bun is growing fast, indeed. The little white blaze on her forehead, a mark that most baby cottontails lose as they grow up, is becoming fainter all the time. As the old man often tells her, by autumn, she'll be a "big-enough bunny," just like her mother and grandmother. But for now, she's still just a little girl, covered nose-to-toes with soft downy baby fur that makes her look like she's wearing fleecy Dr. Denton pajamas.

As Bittiest Bun hops out from beneath the bishop's weed, she is startled by a cold shower of water drops that had clung to the leaves and flowers since last night's big rainstorm.

"That's one sure way to wake up those sleepy little bunny eyes," the old man chuckles.

Bittiest Bun quickly hops out of the perennial bed and onto the lawn. She arches her back and shakes off the water, then sits up and begins wiping her face with her front paws.

"Is any-bunny thinkin' about that ol' cookie and all those big raisins?" asks the old man.

At the sound of the word, "cookie," Bittiest Bun's ears perk up, she stops wiping her face and looks over at the old man.

"Here's that ol' cookie," says the old man, leaning forward across his lap and holding out a piece toward her. "Better hurry up or I just might hafta eat this ol' cookie, myself."

The little rabbit hops toward the old man, pausing just short of his hand. Sniffing the air as she inches forward, Bittiest Bun's nose zeroes in on the cookie's delicious aroma and follows the scent like a bead sliding along a string.

The old man holds the cookie very still as she slowly creeps closer and closer. "Just look at that ol' cookie," he says tantalizingly. "All those s-w-e-e-t, s-o-f-t, c-h-e-w-y raisins. Ummmmm, that ol' cookie's just so good."

Unable to resist any longer, Bittiest Bun slowly, but steadily, stretches forward, keeping eye contact with the old man, until her nose bumps into the cookie. As she takes the cookie gently in her mouth, the old man slowly draws away his hand and leans back in his seat on the stone wall, all the while telling her what an especially good girl she is.

In her first bite, Bittiest Bun gets an exceptionally large raisin and happily savors every sweet chewy bit of it.

Smiling down, the old man asks, "That ol' cookie's just so good, mind if I have some, too?" Helping himself to a piece from his pocket, he smacks his lips and exclaims, "Ummmm, g-o-o-d cookie!"

Looking up as he speaks, Bittiest Bun runs her tiny pink tongue from one corner of her mouth to the other, showing her enthusiastic agreement.

As the two friends enjoy their cookies together, a familiar voice cheerfully calls out from the top of the big ash tree in the middle of the yard: "Pretty, pretty, pretty."

"I hear Mr. Cardinal," says the old man, looking up. "Is that ol' cardinal lookin' for a peanut?"

A bright red male cardinal flits downward, alighting on a branch of the mulberry tree just a few feet above the old man's head. "Stick, stick," replies Mr. Cardinal, leaning forward eagerly on his perch.

"Sure, I've always got a peanut for that ol' cardinal," says the old man. "He's a good neighbor. Yeah, he's one of the good guys, you betcha." Using one finger to sort through several peanuts spread across the palm of his hand, he mutters, "We gotta find a good one, now, a real dandy."

Because a cardinal's beak doesn't open wide enough to fit around a peanut's shell, the old man pinches the dimpled end of a big double-nutter between his thumb and first finger until the shell splits. Then he rolls it side-to-side, until the shell gapes open partly down both sides.

As the peanut shell crackles in the old man's fingers, the cardinal anxiously cranes his neck around some leaves that partially block his view, his tall crest spreading open like a red fan. Then the old man tosses the peanut out on the lawn in a high, lofting arc. Mr. Cardinal flies up and, nearly meeting it in mid-air, follows it down to the ground. First glancing about to be sure that no blue jays or squirrels are near, he bites down on an exposed edge of the split-open shell and darts off through the big vegetable garden, flying fast and low to the ground.

Instantly, Mr. Cardinal's mate flies down from the ash tree and follows closely behind him to the far southwest corner of the old man's garden where they will share a romantic picnic on the ground beneath a thick tangled bower of red wild dogwood shoots and green leafy raspberry canes.

The squirrels, having finished their peanuts, are coming back for seconds. Brazenly striding up behind Bittiest Bun with its tail flicking agitatedly, one of them appears to be thinking about stealing the rest of her cookie.

"Okay, all you fuzzytails, git! Cookies are for bunnies, not squirrels," the old man scolds as he quickly tosses out another peanut to each squirrel.

One squirrel loses sight of her peanut in the grass, but the sharp eyes of a blue jay see it clearly from high up in the ash tree. When the squirrel turns around to search behind her, the jay plummets down and, in the blink of an eye, snatches up the peanut in its beak and vaults back into the air. Sitting up and clutching her front paws to her chest, the squirrel sadly watches the jay fly off.

"Hah, he got you good that time, Fuzzytail," laughs the old man. "Well alright, here's another, then. Catch!"

When he tosses out the second peanut, the squirrel stands up on her hind legs, spreads wide her front paws and stares skyward like a shortstop settling under a pop fly. But the peanut falls between her paws, hits her right on the nose and bounces away.

"E-six on your scorecards, fans!" laughs the old man, slapping his knee with amusement. "Oh man, Fuzzytail, this just isn't your day."

Diving in the direction that the peanut had bounced, the squirrel jabs her nose down into the wet grass and, after sniffing around a bit, comes up with it in her teeth. Turning the peanut end- over-end under her nose with her paws, she checks for any breaks in the shell. Finding none, she decides to bury it for later. Bounding across the lawn to the big vegetable garden, she jumps to the top of its oak split rail fence and then down among the rows of sturdy young broccoli plants.

"Oh no you don't, Fuzzytail," scolds the old man, rising to his feet. "That's a number one, class-A, extra-fancy peanut and you'd better not just go stickin' it in the mud."

By this time, the squirrel is head down, fanny high, digging away madly with both front paws into the soft wet soil and compost heaped up around a broccoli plant. With the peanut clenched in her teeth and front paws flailing away, she's oblivious to the old man.

Striding quickly toward the garden, the old man calls out loudly, "Hey, did you hear me? Get your fuzzy tail out of there!"

Startled, the squirrel stops digging and looks back over her shoulder. When the old man walks still closer, the squirrel scampers down between the rows of broccoli, jumps up on the fence and runs along the top rail to the corner of the garden. There, she hops up to the top of the corner post, sits down with her fluffy tail curled S-like upward over her head and begins tearing into the peanut's shell with her teeth.

"That's better," says the old man as he swings one leg over the fence and, using his boot, pushes the damp soil and compost back up around the broccoli plant and tamps it down.

Starting back toward the house, the old man notices that, after several bites, Little-Bitty Bun has stopped eating her cookie and is munching on clover.

"Washin' down that ol' cookie with a little salad?" he asks her, knowing that cottontails rarely, if ever, drink water, but get their daily fluids from the fresh succulent plants that they eat. "That's a good girl, but now don't forget about the rest of that ol' cookie or somebody else'll get it when you're not lookin'," he warns.

Bittiest Bun has finished all of her cookie and is under the big fir tree with her grandma. Both are grooming. Sitting up tall, Old Mrs. Bun reaches up with both front paws and bends down her long ears, one at a time, brushing each one between her paws all the way to the end. Bittiest Bun just rubs her front paws around and around over her eyes and nose.

As he walks by, the old man bends down and looks in under the fir tree's fragrant needled branches. "All cookied up, Bun?" he asks.

Old Mrs. Bun, lazily scratching behind one ear with a hind foot, pauses in mid-scratch and looks up at him. Two more scratches and she's done. Then, standing stiffly erect on her front legs, she leans forward and stretches out her back legs so far that her belly almost touches the ground, all the while giving a big, long, toothy yawn.

She surveys the ground around her and paws some dead leaves, a small fir cone and a pebble out of the way. Annoyed by a small dead twig hanging down too near her ears, she stands up on her hind legs, bites it off and discards it carefully to one side. Now, she paws the ground rapidly with her front feet and, turning end-for-end, paws the ground some more in the opposite direction.

Old Mrs. Bun sniffs the freshly scratched-up earth, then paws the ground again, as before, first in one direction, then the other. Now, after a second sniff test, she finally seems satisfied and flops with a plop onto her side for a little lie-down.

Bittiest Bun is feeling much too frisky even to think about resting. She races back and forth around the arc of bare earth beneath the skirt of the fir tree, leaping up and kicking out with her back feet at every turn. She just feels so-o-o good.

But Old Mrs. Bun is not amused by all the commotion. She slowly raises her head and gazes blankly at her overly-peppy little granddaughter. When their eyes meet, Bittiest Bun stops right in her tracks. She pauses for a moment, then hops out to the edge of the lawn, just below the ends of the longest branches, to browse quietly on the grass and clover while her grandma rests.

As he takes his seat on the low stone wall, the old man is happy to see that Bittiest Bun has learned to stay near overhead cover as a precaution against large hawks and owls. "That Bittiest Bun's a smart girl," he praises. "Sure, she knows a little bunny needs to stay close to her bush."

I know all the birds on these hills and the teeming wildlife of the fields is in my care.

Psalm 50: 11.

hile the old man tries to find a comfortable seat among the stones atop the wall, he is paged from above by a chorus of tiny pleas for his attention.

"Sweet, sweet," calls the tufted titmouse.

"Tsee-tsee-tsee," pleads the tiny black-capped chickadee.

"I hear that ol' titmouse and that ol' chickadee-dee-dee," he says, looking up. "You guys lookin' for some peanuts, too? Sure."

But, before the old man can get up from his seat, Itchy Bob jumps up onto his knee as if to say, "Wait a minute, me first."

"Okay, Bob, make it snappy," insists the old man, as he holds out a handful of peanuts. Itchy Bob jumps right into the old man's palm and begins picking up and sniffing every peanut.

"Let's not be so fussy, Bob," begs the old man. "You're gettin' to be as persnickety as an old lady at a fruit market."

"Speek, speek," comes another tiny voice from the ash tree.

"And that little downy woodpecker wants some peanuts, too," urges the old man. "Let's go, Bob, hurry it up."

But fickle Itchy Bob is having a hard time making up his mind.

"Greed, greed," rasps the unhappy titmouse.

"Cheat-cheat-cheat," complains the chickadee.

"Okay, Bob," says the old man. "Too much dawdle."

He lowers his hand, Itchy Bob, peanuts and all down to the top of the wall. After Itchy Bob hops down from his hand, the old man places several big double-nutters on the wall for him.

"There you go, Bob," he says. "Now you can take all the time you want, but I've got customers waitin'."

As the old man walks over to the big triple-tube birdfeeder hanging below the ash tree, he whistles loud, echoing the calls of another titmouse out in the little woods beyond the meadow:

[Peter-peter-peter] "Peter-peter-peter"

[Weep-weep-weep] "Weep-weep-weep."

Soon, that titmouse flies to the yard and joins in the clamor for peanuts with the others.

Standing beneath the feeder and shelling peanuts, the old man encourages his small friends. "Here we go, guys. Here we go, now — lotsa peanuts for everybody. Sure, that ol' titmouse and that ol' chickadee-dee-dee get after those peanuts, yeah they do. And that ol' downy woodpecker — sure, he knows what to do. Here we go, guys, lotsa peanuts for everybody."

As the old man continues to shell and split peanuts into halves for his small-beaked friends, they get excited and begin making fly-bys close to the feeder. Two chickadees come in for a closer look and alight on the wire that suspends the feeder. Gripping it with their toes, one foot above the other, they lean out sideways to peek down into the feeder's dish-like bottom tray.

As the titmice grouse loudly to hurry things up, the little downy woodpecker flutters in a slow circle around the feeder, just above the old man's head, then lands on the side of the ash tree. He uses his short stiff tail feathers braced against the tree trunk to prop himself upright as he peeks over his shoulder down at the feeder.

Soon, lots of shelled peanut halves are in the feeder's tray and the little downy can wait no longer. He dives to the feeder. Clinging to the side of the tray by his long toes with only his head showing above the rim, he shuffles sideways around the tray until he spots the peanut he wants. Pulling himself up higher and rocking forward, he snares it in his beak, pushes off backwards into the air, rolls upright and flies back to the trunk of the ash tree.

"Yeah, that ol' downy woodpecker snagged a big one," the old man cheers. "That's the stuff."

The little downy scoots up the tree trunk in short galloping bounds, searching for just the right spot to enjoy his breakfast. Coming to a nearly upright fork in one of the large limbs halfway up the tree, he jambs the peanut into a depression in the "V" between the two branches and begins jackhammering off bite-sized chunks with his stout chisel-like beak.

The chickadees and titmice have flown up high in the trees with their prizes. Perched on branches small enough to wrap their toes around, they hold the peanut halves tightly between their feet while they use their beaks to pry off small pieces.

"That ol' titmouse got a big one," notes the old man. "Yeah, and that ol' chickadee-dee-dee? Sure, he got a big one, too. There you go — that's the stuff, guys."

The old man walks back to his porch for more peanuts and is met there by Shelley, Itchy Bob and two squirrels. "Okay, guys, just a minute'n I'll get some more," he says, stepping in the back door.

Coming back out, he tosses a peanut to each of the squirrels, then kneels down and loads up Shelley and Itchy

Bob with three big double-nutters, each. His cheeks full and his spitter in place, Itchy Bob turns and sprints down the flagstones toward the lawn, but suddenly stops. One of the squirrels is eating its peanut atop the short stout log that the old man stood up on its end near the porch for use as a chopping block when splitting firewood. The squirrel is sitting at the edge of the log with his tail curled upward and its back turned toward Itchy Bob. Bob is powerless to resist such an inviting target for a prank.

Quickly scampering to the chopping block and up its side to a spot just below the squirrel's tail, Itchy Bob jabs his cold nose right into the squirrel's private business. The shocked squirrel bolts high into the air, turning a crazy, legs-flailing, partial back somersault before landing awkwardly on its head deep within the thick foliage of the shady perennial flower bed.

"Aw gee, Bob, aren't you ever going to grow up?" scolds the old man, stifling a chuckle. "That wasn't at all nice."

Itchy Bob pauses at the top of the chopping block for a moment to savor his joke, then quickly makes his escape toward the big fir tree at the corner of the house before the squirrel can figure out who's responsible for its humiliation.

Now, beneath the fir tree, Itchy Bob encounters Old Mrs. Bun. She has just sat up from her peaceful repose and is rearranging her resting place when he comes barreling along toward her on a collision course. Surprised, at the last second she hops upward as if skipping rope, and Itchy Bob runs right under her. Bob stops, turns and looks back wide-eyed at Old Mrs. Bun as she stares at him in dismay.

"Don't even think about it, Bob," warns the old man.

But, Bob's not listening — he's thinking, "Wow, cool!" As quick as a wink, he runs back and makes the bunny jump again. Now, Old Mrs. Bun has her dander up. A joke is a joke, but enough is enough.

"Uh-oh, Bob, now you've done it," cautions the old man. "You'd better find a different route home."

As usual, Itchy Bob's not listening. Always one to push a good thing too far, he figures he's on a roll and that just once more can't hurt. But, as he takes a run toward Old Mrs. Bun for the third time, she sits back on her haunches and puts up her dukes. Realizing too late that she's not going to hop up and out of his way, Itchy Bob screeches to a halt just as Old Mrs. Bun unloads on him. Boxing with both front paws as a kangaroo might, she lands a quick one-two combination of left jab and short right cross to the chin that sends him crashing backward to the ground and his spitter flying.

"Bingo!" shouts the old man with a laugh.

Itchy Bob gets up, shakes his head and stares unsteadily up at Old Mrs. Bun in utter disbelief. Suddenly, as if just remembering something that he's forgot to do, Bob scampers off, this time going wide around the old rabbit.

"Well, Bun, you're still the champ," proclaims the old man. "One of these days that little chip-monkey's gonna wise up — maybe, if he lives long enough."

As Old Mrs. Bun settles back into her resting place, the old man picks up several pieces of peanut shell from off the porch and tosses them out into the shady perennial flower bed. Glancing west out over the meadow, his eye catches sight of a pale shadow in the high grass. "I think I see another cookie customer," he calls out. "Is any-bunny out there thinking about that ol' cookie?"

Two tall rabbit ears peak up above the grass and turn toward the old man. Then a head, rising slowly, appears below the ears.

"Sure, I thought so," says the old man. "There's that Little Bun — he's a cookie boy." Reaching into his pocket for a cookie, the old man steps off the porch and walks out toward the little stream.

As Little Bun, a three-year-old son of Old Mrs. Bun, sits up tall in the high meadow grass, slight chewing-like motions of his jaws tell the old man that this rabbit's very interested in a cookie.

"Well, you gonna get after this ol' cookie, or what?" asks the old man as he arrives at the stream bank. "Hippity-hop, let's go!"

Needing no further encouragement, Little Bun canters out of the high grass, leaps the stream and lands within arm's length of the kneeling old man.

"There's my big guy," declares the old man proudly.

Little Bun stands erect on his hind legs to take his cookie from the old man's hand, then crouches down on the mossy streambank and attacks it with gusto.

"That Little Bun's just so-o-o hungry," exclaims the old man. "Hoo-wee! He's gettin' after that ol' cookie, right now!"

As Little Bun happily chews up big mouthfuls of cookie, the old man sits down on the bank and reaches into his pocket. "Just look what I've got to wash down that ol' cookie — can I interest you in a big, cool, sweet, juicy grape?" he asks, tantalizingly.

Little Bun's ears perk forward and his eyes grow wide at the mention of the word "grape." He leans in closer to the old man and sniffs at his coat sleeve.

"I thought so. I know that Little Bun digs grapes," says the old man, holding up a big, plump, white seedless grape in his fingertips.

Staring intently at the grape, Little Bun quickly finishes a bite of cookie and swallows with a gulp. As the old man holds the grape out toward Little Bun's mouth, the hungry rabbit leans in and carefully bites off half, then sits back and begins to chew.

A rabbit's mouth is not made to handle all the juice in a big ripe grape, but Little Bun is determined to get all that he can. As he chews, he flicks his tongue all around, slurping up the cool sweet liquid as it cascades out the sides of his mouth. Despite his best efforts, much of the juice runs down his chin and jaw.

"That's okay, that's okay," says the old man, chuckling. "We don't give points for neatness."

Finishing the last of the grape, Little Bun laps up a drop or two of juice still clinging to his whiskers and burps before finishing off his last bite of cookie.

"Is that better? All cookied up?" asks the old man as Little Bun sits up and demonstrates proper rabbit etiquette by wiping his mouth and chin with his paws. Like a man adjusting his belt after a big supper, Little Bun accommodates his meal by stretching out his stomach and hind legs rearward while leaning far forward on stiffly straight front legs. He sniffs the ground to be sure he hasn't overlooked any cookie crumbs.

"Such a big strong guy!" boasts the old man, proudly. "And did I mention handsome? Yessiree, he's a dandy-lookin' bunny!"

Little Bun sniffs the toe of the old man's boot, stares up at his face briefly, then turns, bounds over the stream and lopes back out into the meadow.

"Seeya later, ol' buddy," calls out the old man as he gets up to his knees. Rising slowly, the old man uses one hand braced on top of his knee, to push himself upward. Now standing, he quietly sighs as the stiffness in his back starts to works free.

A sudden burst of "tch-tch-tch-tch-tch-tch-tch-tch," like the sound of caracas being shaken vigorously, comes from high up in the quartet of pine trees at the northwest corner of the yard. That's where the old man hangs birdhouses for some of his smallest feathered friends. Looking up and walking fast toward the sound, he sees a squirrel come bursting out through the pine needles, its legs churning madly in empty air. Something has run it right off the end of a branch about ten feet above the ground.

The squirrel face-plants in a heap on the ground. Dizzily, it shakes its head a few times and, without looking back, jumps up and takes off running as fast as it can, north into the next-door neighbor's backyard.

A tiny, grayish-brown dart-of-a-bird dives from the pine branches, straight down, and levels off sharply at the grass tops. Little Mrs. House Wren's wings are just blurs as she pursues the squirrel like a heat-seeking missile, skimming across the yard only inches above the ground. Hopping mad, she's buzzing like a rattlesnake and flying as fast as a bullet.

As it flees, zig-zagging crazily across the yard, the squirrel curls its fleecy tail up and forward over its back like a canopy to shield its head from the angry mother's beak. But it apparently hasn't had time to consider all the consequences of this strategy. While protecting its head, the squirrel has left itself vulnerable, or to be more accurate, very much exposed, to a different kind of attack.

Despite all of the squirrel's evasive maneuvers, it is quickly overtaken by little Mrs. House Wren and her sharp, almost inch-long, needle-like beak. Sizing up her target for maximum effect, she immediately spots the most glaring weakness in the squirrel's defense. Zooming in low, she nails its unprotected fanny so hard that its back feet are lifted high over its head and it runs the next twenty feet on its front legs alone.

"Holy cow!" shouts the old man, just exploding with laughter. "Oooooh-weee," he gasps through clenched teeth, his eyes squinting tightly and his mouth scrunching up as if he had just bit into a very sour lemon.

"Oh wow, man, that's really gotta smart," he chuckles, trying his best to strike a sympathetic note. "That's one ol' fuzzytail who won't be sittin' down anytime soon. No-o-o-o way!"

Satisfied that the squirrel has been taught that trespassing will not be tolerated, Mrs. Wren returns to the pine tree and alights on the roof of a small birdhouse hanging from the branch that the squirrel had so hastily evacuated. Not yet calmed down, she does a defiant little foot-stomping dance while chattering out a loud warning to anyone else who might think about coming near her family's home.

"Atta girl, Mrs. Wren!" the old man calls up to her, pumping his fist. "You sure tattooed that ol' fuzzytail's nosy little hooha, but good. Atta girl, atta girl!"

When Mr. Wren arrives at the birdhouse with his beak full of insects, Mrs. Wren cools down enough to follow him inside and tend to their loudly chirping hungry nestlings.

Walking back toward his house and still chuckling to himself over the nosy squirrel's comeuppance, the old man notices lots of tiny yellow blossoms in his lawn. Kneeling down and examining the little flowers more closely, he happily predicts, "Well, it won't be long now til all those dandy little bunnies'll be grazin' belly deep on wild strawberries. Nope, won't be long, at all."

Mischief does not grow out of the soil, nor trouble spring from the earth.

Job 5: 6.

hile some people's lawns look like flat, short-cropped green carpets, the old man's grass is tall-mowed at 3 1/2 inches high and is colorfully crowded with white clover, dandelions, violets, lambs-quarters and other natural plants and wild flowers that many people think of as weeds. But, if you happen to be a rabbit, the old man's lawn is a delightful buffet of fragrant aromas, sweet flavors and succulent textures that is just irresistibly delicious.

There are lots of things at the old man's garden that his bird and animal friends like, but what it does not have is very important, too. Some of the chemicals that people spray on their gardens and lawns as fertilizer or to kill weeds and bugs can harm small animals and birds and kill insects that are helpful in the garden, like ladybugs, lacewings and honey bees.

So, there are no herbicides, pesticides or chemical fertilizers used anywhere in the old man's garden. His lawn, flowers and vegetable plots are all strictly organic to make sure that all the good things that his bird and animal friends find there are safe for them to eat.

Although his rabbit friends enjoy eating many of the natural plants and wild flowers that grow in his lawn, there are some plants that neither the old man nor the rabbits welcome. So, when he spots obnoxious sorts like garlic, sedge or thistle in his lawn, he simply pulls them out, roots and all.

As for unwanted insects, the old man relies on his many bird friends to take care of them. In spring and summer when vegetables and flowers are growing, the birds are raising families. Everyone knows how hungry baby birds are — they never get filled up. And, what do baby birds eat? Big juicy bugs, caterpillars and worms! So, when their nestlings squawk for food, the parent birds know where to find what they need.

Purple finches, house finches and house sparrows like to hunt for bugs in big groups. Lining up in long rows along the split rail fences around the old man's vegetable gardens, they all jump off together, feet-first like paratroopers, right down in among the plants. Happily chattering and chirping away to each other as they hop around from leaf to stem snatching up bugs and caterpillars, they seem to have as much fun as little kids enjoying the swings, slide and monkey bars at a playground.

Other birds do it differently. Cardinals work alone or with their mates as they scout through the plants, top to bottom. Tiny house wrens, larger Carolina wrens and song sparrows also work alone or in mated pairs, searching the bottom parts of the plants, peeking under low-hanging leaves and probing through the clutter of dead leaves and compost beneath the plants. Robins are strictly solo acts as they patrol along the ground probing the soil and occasionally jumping up to nab a bug from off an overhanging leaf.

All day long, the parent birds fly back-and-forth, back-and-forth, between their nests and the old man's gardens, trying to catch enough insects, grubs, caterpillars and worms to keep up with the appetites of their nestlings. And, they don't patrol just the vegetable and flower gardens. The whole crew, from the largest red-bellied woodpeckers, flickers and brown thrashers to the smallest finches, wrens and chickadees, work hard to keep the old man's vegetables, flowers, lawn, trees and bushes clean of insects.

To thank the birds for all that they do for him, the old man fills his many feeders with their favorite seeds and makes sure that there's always plenty of fresh water for drinking and bathing. There are four big birdbaths in his yard that get hosed out and filled up every day. On really hot days, they sometimes have to be filled three or four times to keep up with the heavy traffic of birds, squirrels and chipmunks who come by to cool off and wet their whistles.

Security is important, too. We all want to feel safe in our homes and neighborhoods and birds are no different. For the smaller birds who often have a hard time finding good places to build their nests, the old man puts up birdhouses that are hard for nest robbers to get into. And, he doesn't allow predators like black snakes, hawks, owls, crows, dogs or cats in his yard — especially not cats. Because they're stealthy, quick and good climbers, cats are one of the worst enemies that birds and small animals have. If any of those guys come around, the old man sends them scooting, in a hurry.

A friend is a companion through all things,
and a brother is born to share troubles.

Proverbs 17: 17.

rriving back at his porch from witnessing the nosy squirrel's educational adventure with little Mrs. House Wren, the old man takes down his hose from the side of his tool shed and washes out and fills up the birdbaths until they overflow like cool, sparkling fountains. Then, putting away the hose, he gets out his work gloves and follows the flagstone path out to the big vegetable garden. It's time for work.

With puddles here and there from last night's rain, the garden's too muddy to hoe, so the old man walks around the outside of the fence inspecting his vegetables. Before he gets very far, here come Itchy Bob and Shelley, down from the back porch, bounding along from flagstone to flagstone as they race toward him.

Reaching the garden fence, the chipmunks climb up a corner post and run along the top rail to where the old man is.

"More peanuts? Okay, here we go," he says as he puts several on the top of a fencepost. "But be quick, I've got work to do."

As the old man leans over the fence to check the head of a big broccoli plant, the two chipmunks begin to squabble over first pick of the peanuts.

"Hey you guys," calls out the old man. "Let's remember our manners, huh? Be nice, now."

Shelley, being the polite one, backs off and Itchy Bob assumes control of the pile. When Bob takes his usual long time choosing which peanuts to take, the old man reaches into his pocket and motions to Shelley to come to him. She runs along the top rail to him and quickly stows away the two cheeks and a spitter that he gives her. Shelley jumps down from the fence and is back on the flagstone path on her way home to her burrow before Itchy Bob can decide which peanut to take first.

Watching Itchy Bob and his peanuts with a larcenous eye from up in the ash tree is Jasper, the blue jay. To get a better look, he flies over into the big fir tree at the corner of the house. Seeing the jay enter the tree, the old man mutters to himself, "Oh, oh, Jasper that's a big mistake. You know that tree's off limits for you — it's too close to the catbirds' nest."

Before the old man can finish his observation, Mr. Catbird flies into the fir tree to confront the trespassing jay. Neither the catbird nor the old man have noticed that another blue jay is silently perched higher in the fir tree, up near the top.

"Eee-yeah! Eee-yeah!" snarls the catbird at Jasper.

"That 'ol catbird's fixin' to rip out a few of your tail feathers, Jasper," warns the old man. "You'd better sky-up outa there fast, or you'll be wearin' him like an ugly sweater."

But Jasper just plays it cool. Only scornfully glancing over at the catbird, he pays him no heed at all.

The catbird moves in closer. "Eee-yeah!" he repeats, with fire in his eyes, his slate gray feathers bristling and his black cap raised.

"He's not bluffin,' Jasper," calls out the old man. "You'd better git while the gittin's good."

But instead, the jay makes a threatening hop toward the catbird and angrily rebukes him, "Skaaa!"

His warnings having failed to resolve the situation without a fight, the catbird lunges in. As the two birds go at it, the second jay quickly drops down from the top of the tree and joins in with Jasper, two against one.

Its greater size and large powerful beak make a blue jay a real handful for a catbird under the best of circumstances, but fighting off two jays at once is a very dangerous predicament.

The three angry birds instantly meld into a tight furious knot of grasping feet, flailing wings and snapping beaks. With all screaming fiercely, the unruly ball of squalling birds careens crazily from branch to branch down through the fir tree like a marble in a pinball machine. The overmatched catbird, though fighting valiantly for his family, clearly is getting the worst of it.

Suddenly, a bright bolt of brilliant red streaks out from the small woods beyond the meadow, over the big vegetable garden and right into the fir tree. Flying as fast and straight as an arrow, Mr. Cardinal's heard the ruckus and has come to even up the odds.

Without slowing, the cardinal slams into the tangle of fighting birds, instantly breaking the blue jays' hold on the catbird. The tide is quickly turned. In a short ferocious battle, paired off one-on-one, the cardinal and catbird give the two jays far more than they can handle. The jays' once-savage war cries quickly turn into frantic screams of desperation.

Bursting out of the fir tree, as if their tail feathers were on fire, the jays beat a hasty retreat from the old man's garden, south, toward a distant big woods.

Flying together, side-by-side, the triumphant cardinal and catbird pursue the blue jays closely for a short distance. When it's clear that the jays are fleeing for their lives, the victors abandon the chase and separate. As if on cue, Mr. Catbird turns left sharply to return to his family's nest, while Mr. Cardinal breaks off crisply to the right, flying back out toward the small woods from where he'd come.

"That's the stuff, guys," calls out the old man, proudly, looking up as the catbird and cardinal pass overhead. "That's how good neighbors pitch in together when trouble comes. Outta sight!"

You will laugh at violence and starvation and have no need to fear wild beasts; for you have a covenant with the stones to spare your fields, and the weeds have been constrained to leave you at peace.

Job 5: 22-23.

ld Mrs. Bun, disturbed from her rest by the birds' commotion, has come out from under the big fir tree. She follows the flagstone path, ambling along in an easy, rocking, hobbyhorse-like gait down the walkway between the split rail fences that surround both the big vegetable garden and, alongside it, the smaller pole bean garden.

As the flagstone path nears the south ends of the two fenced gardens, it divides briefly to accommodate the trunk of an apple tree that stands there. Once past the apple tree, the walkway rejoins and leads past the heaped up mound of the sweet potato plot, finally ending at the woodchip-mulched strawberry patch and red raspberry trellises that fill the southwest corner of the yard.

The area along the walkway between the two garden fences is one of Old Mrs. Bun's favorite summertime spots. There, she can lie in the sun to get warm or cool off in the shade of the apple tree. She often spends hours there, moving from sunshine to shade, and back again, as it suits her.

She especially likes being there when the old man's working in his garden, so she can let down her guard against dogs, cats and big hawks. She knows she's safe from those dangers when he's close by. With her eyes closed, Old Mrs. Bun relies on the sound of his voice, his slow, heavy footsteps and the rhythmic "chink-chink-chink" of his hoe to reassure her.

Cottontails don't often get to kick back. They're at the top of many predators' menus, so they have to be on their guard all the time. Relaxing usually means crouching down low in concealing foliage with feet poised beneath them for a fast getaway. It's not very restful, but it's preferable to becoming somebody's supper.

Old Mrs. Bun hasn't lived as long as she has by being careless. Even when she appears to be asleep, she's very alert. Her eyes are seldom fully shut and her long ears, rotating from front to back either together or independently, continually monitor all the sounds around her, especially the calls of birds whose sharp eyes rarely fail to discover the approach of a dangerous intruder.

Now, as she lies in the sun next to the garden fence, the everyday chitchat and gossip of the birds and the sounds of the old man as he works around his garden, allow Old Mrs. Bun enough security to truly relax — so she embraces the opportunity.

Rolling onto her back, she stretches out her back legs to one side and her front legs out to the opposite side. She leans back her head until her chin points skyward, exhales gently and slowly closes her eyes.

"Well, that's not very ladylike, Bun," teases the old man playfully as he peeks over at her. Old Mrs. Bun's eyes slowly roll open and gaze up lazily at him for a moment, then drift closed again.

The old man gently eases himself down to the ground beside the sweet potato plot and begins slowly and methodically pulling up all the tiny weeds and sprigs of grass that have grown up among the young sparsely-leafed sprouts during the two weeks' time since they were set into the ground.

"Gotta get after these little guys, Bun, before they get big and start to crowd these ol' sweet potatoes," he says. "After a good rain they pull up real easy — yessir, and with all their roots, too."

As the old man pulls weeds, he hums softly to himself and, now and then, exchanges greetings with various birds and chipmunks who stop by. Old Mrs. Bun hears it all as she lazes nearby in the grass, occasionally changing position and drifting in and out of sleep.

After a long while that seems like only minutes, the old man slowly gets up to his feet. "Lunchtime, Bun," he announces.

Now lying on her side in the shade of the apple tree, Old Mrs. Bun lifts her head and looks up at the old man as he passes by.

"I think this ol' ground has finally warmed up enough to plant pole beans this afternoon," he says as he walks up the flagstones toward the house. "It's good we got the ground tilled and the poles put up before that rain. Shouldn't be too muddy — a little bit more sunshine and it should be just about right."

With the old man leaving, Old Mrs. Bun gets up to her feet, stretches and resumes her regular vigil. Between glances around, she nibbles on sweet blossoms of white clover that have grown tall close to the trunk of the apple tree.

Little-Bitty Bun welcomes you to the old man's garden.

Old Mrs. Bun blissfully savors a bite of raisin from her breakfast cookie.

Bittiest Bun emerges from the perennial bed beneath the little fan-shaped mulberry tree.

Little Bun responds on the run to the old man's call at "cookie time."

Fatty has a cool splash in the birdbath beneath the little fan-shaped mulberry tree.

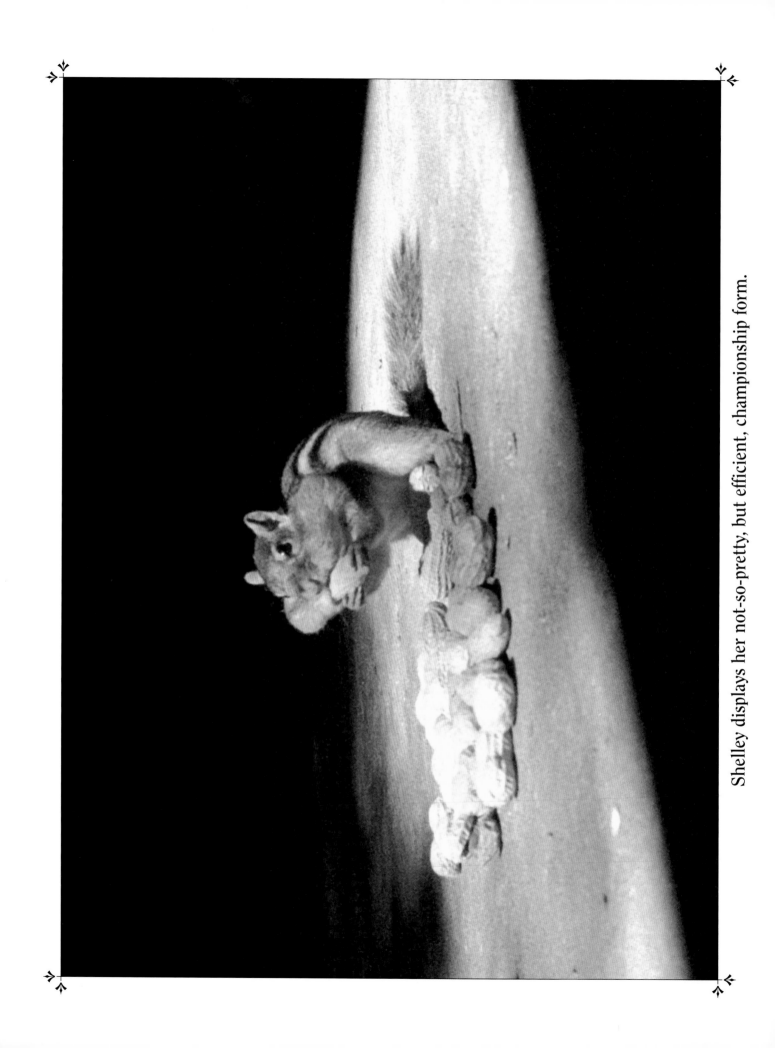

Shelley displays her not-so-pretty, but efficient, championship form.

Itchy Bob loads up on peanuts while planning his next bit of adventure.

Thoreau ("Speedy") gets a good grip on his spitter before heading home to his burrow.

Behold, how good it is, and how pleasant, for brothers to live together in unity!

Psalm 133: 1.

he old man brings out his lunch to the porch on a tray and sets it on a small table. He pulls up a big thick-cushioned chair, bends slowly and sits down with an abrupt plop. With effort, he pulls off his garden boots and puts them beside his chair. A long low sigh escapes his smile as he wriggles his toes inside his socks and rubs the soles of his feet on the porch's cool concrete surface. He takes a short sip of cold lemonade, followed by a longer one. Slipping his arms out of his coat, he settles it around the back of his chair and rolls up his shirt sleeves two turns, to just below the elbow.

As the old man reaches for his plate, Itchy Bob jumps up onto the table. "Nice of you to join me for lunch, Bob," quips the old man, setting his plate on his lap. "Is there anything in particular I can get you? Potato chip? Pickle?"

Reaching behind him, and down, the old man takes several peanuts out of his coat pocket and places them on the porch next to his boots. "There you go," he says. "I think that'll be more to your liking. Bon appetit."

Itchy Bob jumps from the table onto the old man's knee, then slides down his pants leg to his foot. Hopping down to the porch, he begins examining the peanuts, sniffing and sizing each one.

The old man takes a bite of his sandwich, stuffs in a potato chip and leans back in his chair, chewing slowly and letting his gaze rove slowly around his yard. At the wood pile just off the porch, two juvenile chipmunks are playing.

"Hey you little chip-monkey babies," he calls out. "Did your mamas drop you off at day-care, today?"

At the sound of the old man's voice, the young chipmunks pause and look over at him, then resume their play.

Looking down for Itchy Bob, the old man sees him scamper off, his cheeks bulging with peanuts. As Bob runs, the peanuts rattle in their shells, sounding the cadence of his bounds.

"Watch out for that cat," teases the old man.

Itchy Bob pauses just long enough to give the old man a mildly annoyed backward glance, then continues on his way.

Chewing up the last bite of his sandwich, the old man reaches into his pants pocket, takes out his pocketknife and opens out its sharp shiny blade. He picks up an apple from his lunch tray and rubs it against his flannel shirt until it glosses bright red, then begins to peel it. Turning the apple around and around in his hands while holding it against the knife blade, he's making one long, continuous, curly strand of apple peeling.

As he peels the apple, the old man hears a faint "clickety-click" noise from the gravel surrounding the porch and looks left, toward the sound.

"Hey, Bun," he says. "Decide to come in? Sure, that ol' sun's gettin' pretty warm out there. Come on up here to the shade where its cooler."

Old Mrs. Bun totters across the gravel, up onto the porch, and comes over to the old man's lunch table. Sitting up tall with her front paws held close to her chest for balance, she stares wide-eyed at the long, shiny coil of peel dangling from the apple and wriggles her nose with interest. As the old man continues with his work, the shiny red apple peel accordions up and down and slowly twirls in front of Old Mrs. Bun's eyes with almost hypnotic effect. She stands up on her hind legs, leans in and pushes out her nose toward the dancing peel to get a sniff.

"Apple? Think you'd like to try a piece of apple?" asks the old man. "Sure, we can do that — just a minute."

He raises his hands high and swings the peel over his lunch tray as he makes the last cut, dropping the whole long coil onto his empty plate. He cuts the peeled apple in half, then quarters it.

Removing the core from one quarter, he cuts off a small slice and holds it out to Old Mrs. Bun. She sniffs it once, twice, and then sits down and licks her lips.

"Well, whatcha think, Bun? Is that some kinda dandy or what?" asks the old man.

Old Mrs. Bun licks her lips again, then sits back up and slowly takes the slice of apple in her mouth. Coming down on all fours, she has a quizzical look on her face. She crouches down on the porch, takes a small bite and begins chewing slowly, then faster. She takes another bite, a big one — then, another.

"Pretty good, huh? asks the old man. "Different from the little green ones you find under the apple tree — a whole lot sweeter and juicier, huh."

Old Mrs. Bun chews up and swallows her last bite of apple. She sits up and wipes her mouth with her front paws then pulls her chin to her collarbone and briefly licks clean the brisket fur just below her throat. Finished, she looks up at the old man contentedly.

"A little bit of okay, huh Bun?" he asks her. "Sure, I bet that Ol' Bun's gonna be an apple girl, now."

The old man leans far back in his chair and leisurely carves off a slice of apple and, using the knife blade like a server and his thumb as a pusher, slides it into his mouth. He slowly chews up the first crunchy slice and swallows. "Ahhh," he sighs. "No better dessert on a summer day than a cool, crisp, juicy apple — that's a fact."

Old Mrs. Bun ambles slowly over to a spot near the edge of the porch where the concrete is still damp and shaded by the little mulberry tree, and flops down lazily on her side. She doesn't budge even a little bit, but only slightly twitches one long ear to shoo away a gnat that flies too near.

Looking over at her and smiling, the old man asks, "Is this livin' or what, Bun?"

As the old man slides another apple slice off the knife blade into his mouth, Shelley comes from the ground cover on the north side of the house, skitters over the gravel up onto the porch and crosses behind the old man's chair. Sticking very close at her side is another chipmunk, a tiny bit smaller, somewhat thinner and only slightly paler in color.

The two continue across the porch, past the old man's tool shed, and stop to drink side-by-side from the birdbath on the gravel beneath the branches of the big fir tree. As they drink, they pause and, together, take note of their surroundings, looking first here, then there. After another sip, they hop down from the birdbath and move on, disappearing around the corner of the house.

"Well, Bun, looks like Shelley's showin' the ropes to another of her little chip-monkey babies, today," remarks the old man as he slowly chews up another slice of apple. "She's such a good mama. Most of 'em just turn their kids loose on their own when they're old enough. Not her — she even helps 'em dig their burrows and stock up food for winter. Yessir, she's just amazin' — a real sweetie."

After the old man finishes his last slice of apple, he carefully wipes the blade of his knife on his trouser leg, folds it up and slides it into his pocket. He drinks the last of his lemonade, picks up his lunch tray and goes into the house. In a moment, he comes back out with a re-filled glass and a newspaper under his arm. Sitting down, he pulls out his old blue bandanna and shakes it free of lint.

As he slowly wipes off his eyeglasses, the old man notices that Old Mrs. Bun has left the porch and crossed the stream over to the meadow side. After nibbling on a few buds of red clover, she ambles toward the cover and shade of the little woods, beyond.

"See you later, Bun," he calls out to her. Old Mrs. Bun pauses to rotate one tall ear in the old man's direction. Then, without looking back, she continues toward the tree line.

Sitting back in his chair, the old man opens his newspaper and puts on his glasses. Before he can get beyond the headlines, Shelley and her little shadow return back around the corner of the house and scamper up to the porch. Shelley hops up onto one of the old man's boots beside his chair, with the smaller chipmunk timidly concealing itself behind her.

"There's my little Shelley," says the old man, warmly. "Who's that you've got with you, today, one of your new little babies?"

Shelley turns to the little chipmunk and, with urging that the old man can't hear, calls it forward. But the little chipmunk only peeks shyly out from behind her mother.

"Oh my, she's a bashful one," observes the old man.

Again, Shelley offers silent encouragement and, cautiously, the little chipmunk comes up onto the toe of the boot and huddles close to her mother.

Shelley looks up at the old man, down at the little one, and back up at the old man, as if making a formal introduction.

As the little one meekly peeks up at the old man, Shelley gives her a warm reassuring glance.

"That's sure a pretty little baby you've got there, Shelley," coos the old man. "Oh, she's a dandy, for sure. And she's mighty lucky to have such a good mama as you are."

Shelley's eyes glow with pride as the little one cuddles up close against her, bashfully burying her face in her mother's soft comforting fur and managing only one quick peek upward.

"What shall we call her? asks the old man, looking puzzled. "Hmmm, since you live over by Mr. and Mrs. Pape's house, we could call her Poppy — like the pretty little flower. Whatta you think?"

Beaming up at the old man, Shelley seems pleased.

"Well then, Poppy it is," he says. "Oh, that's a dandy name for such a pretty little girl."

As Shelley and Poppy jump down from the boot and start for home, the old man calls after them, "Nice to meet you, Poppy. Come back soon."

The old man finishes off his lemonade and looks at his watch. "Oops, gettin' late — gotta get back to work if we're gonna get those ol' pole beans planted today," he mutters to himself, reaching down for his boots.

O Lord, who savest both man and beast, how precious is thy unfailing love.

Psalm 36: 7.

efore heading back to the garden, the old man trades his tall rubber garden boots for work shoes. He puts some water in a bucket and dumps in a large envelope of brown pole beans, to soak.

He takes his rake from the tool shed out to the sweet potato plot and sits down where he stopped his morning's work. In a few hours more, the sweet potatoes are clean of all weeds and grass.

"There you go," says the old man. "Now, you ol' sweet potatoes have got some elbow room."

With a few long, sweeping strokes of the rake, he gathers all the pulled-up weeds and grass into a pile and carries it over to the composter drum near the raspberry trellises. Dumping in the pile and giving the drum a few spins to mix the contents, he pleads, "Now, let's see you turn into somethin' good for my garden."

Along the flagstone path between the two fenced gardens, the old man puts down the rake and picks up his osage orange planting stick from off its pegs in the top rail of the fence around the big vegetable garden.

Reaching over the bean garden's fence, he pushes the pointed end of the stick into the ground near the base of one of the tripods of bamboo bean poles. It goes in easily and pulls out cleanly like a toothpick stuck into a cake that has baked just long enough.

"Lookin' good," says the old man. "Lets plant beans."

As he bends to pull out a little weed from the bean garden, a small fluttering form circles above him, once, then twice.

"Uh-oh," says the old man. "I think somebody wants peanuts."

"Speek, speek," replies the little downy woodpecker as he alights on the top of the nearest tripod of bean poles.

"I thought so," scolds the old man, jovially. "You've just gotta have more peanuts, huh? Well, okay, we can do that."

The old man leans the planting stick against the fence, picks up the rake and walks toward the big birdfeeder hanging beneath the ash tree, the little downy woodpecker flying on ahead of him.

At the feeder, the old man has just begun to shell peanuts when he's startled to see Old Mrs. Bun and Little-Bitty Bun leap over the stream from the meadow and race up to his feet. Something's very wrong. Old Mrs. Bun, always quite calm and unflappable, appears anxious, almost pleading, as she looks up at him. Little-Bitty Bun is trembling and her eyes are wide with fright as she stares back out over the meadow.

Following along Little-Bitty Bun's line of sight, the old man spots three robins in the distance, near the top of a low hill. The robins are on the attack, swooping in short steep dives at a large dark object in the grass directly below them.

The old man crosses the stream and hurries toward the little hill in the meadow, followed closely by Little-Bitty Bun. While running, he sees the dark object in the grass leap up suddenly and snap at the swooping robins, "Caaaaw!" It's a huge crow!

Alighting again, the crow bends forward and pecks hard at the ground, pulling up and tossing aside a beakful of dried grass and light fluffy fur. "Oh, no!" gasps the old man, realizing that the crow has found Little-Bitty Bun's burrow and is after her babies.

Running as fast as he can, he waves his arms, shouts and claps his hands hard to make loud popping noises like gunshots, hoping to scare away the crow. The crow looks up, startled, then quickly pushes its huge black beak deep into the burrow.

"Git outta there!" yells the old man, angrily. "Git! Git!"

The robins continue their attack on the crow, but the crow is many times their size and very determined.

When the old man is still about thirty feet away, the crow suddenly straightens up, grasping a baby rabbit in its beak. Taking a quick glance toward the old man, the crow tosses back its head and snaps its beak, getting a better grip on the baby rabbit.

With a muffled, but defiant, "Caw!" the crow leaps up into the air and begins to fly away, north, with three enraged robins in hot pursuit. The robins close in, tightening the circle of their attack. They're all over the crow now, diving, pecking and screaming at it.

Dodging three angry robins, the crow is having a difficult time gaining altitude, but with every long powerful beat of its huge black glistening wings it steadily rises higher and higher into the sky and is picking up speed.

"Git him, guys! Git him!" shouts the old man to the robins as he runs along behind and below the battling birds.

Short of breath, the old man stumbles to a stop and looks up, gasping. Now that his eyeglasses have stopped bouncing, he sees something that he hadn't noticed before. One of the robins in the chase has a long feather sticking up curiously from its back.

"It's that ol' fat robin!" murmurs the old man to himself excitedly. "Git him, Fatty! Git him! Don't let him get away!" he shouts as he begins running again.

With every moment that passes, the crow rises higher in the sky and further ahead of the old man. The situation is desperate and if something doesn't change very quickly, the little baby rabbit will be gone forever.

While his two comrades continue swooping and pecking at the crow, Fatty suddenly veers skyward, straining his wings for altitude. Higher and higher he climbs, until he is far, far above all the others.

Then, peeking downward over his shoulder to locate the crow, Fatty rolls sharply to his left, folds back his wings, rearward like a jet fighter plane, and dives.

Down, down, straight down Fatty streaks. Faster, faster and faster he comes, with the sharp point of his beak stretched out in front of him. Using only his tail and trailing wing tips to adjust his aim, Fatty narrows his eyes, locking onto his target with the steely resolve of a guardian angel in full battle mode. Then....

KA-BAM!!! Fatty slams into the crow like a lightning bolt, driving his beak hard into the crow's back, right between its wings.

Loose feathers, big black ones and small brown ones, fill the air as if a pillow had exploded.

Both of the crow's huge wings shoot straight up as its body is punched hard downward. It's head jerks violently backward and its heavy black beak gapes wide open, letting out a terrible scream of angry defiance ... and losing its grip on the baby rabbit.

For a moment, the old man stops and stares up in pure wonder and awe. "Holy cow, Fatty!" he says quietly to himself. "Holy cow!" He can hardly believe what he has seen.

Then, leaping up and punching the air hard with his fist, the old man shouts aloud, "You got him, Fatty! You got him! You beautiful ol' battlin' fatman, you did it!"

Holding his breath, the old man watches as the baby rabbit plummets toward the ground below. For an almost endless moment, it somersaults silently against the bright pale blue backdrop of sky. Then, it lands like a fluffy tennis ball, gently bouncing once on the thick cushioning nap of lush green meadow grass and softly settling.

"Oh, man, this is one for the books," the old man mutters as he begins to run again, faster than ever. "Holy cow!"

But the battle isn't over. After recoiling from Fatty's blow, the crow makes another try for the baby rabbit. But this time, the old man is much closer than before — too close. And now the robin posse seems to have got its second wind. With three irate robins furiously pelting him like a Kansas hailstorm and the old man closing in fast, the crow gives up and flees.

Running up to where the baby rabbit landed in the grass, the old man stops, leans forward with his hands on his knees and tries to catch his breath. He looks up gratefully to the robins as they chase the crow far out of the meadow. Their fury hasn't yet cooled down and they're still delivering punishment, striking sharp blows from all angles as the dodging crow tries to make its escape.

"That's the stuff guys, smite him hip and thigh!" he hollers out after them. "Take him to school!"

Then peering down, the old man searches for the baby rabbit.

Afraid of stepping on it by accident, he stands still in one place, until he spots the little guy. Crawling clumsily through the deep grass, trying to get away from the bright sunlight and strange sounds, the baby rabbit squeals, "Eeee, eeee, eeee."

The old man kneels down and slowly parts the thick grass with his hands. "You're a mighty lucky little bunny, junior," says the old man softly. "Let's have a good look at you."

Carefully picking up the little rabbit, he runs the tip of one finger along its back, then gently lifts and moves each leg, checking for dislocated or broken bones. Finding none, he examines its nose, ears and mouth and combs through its fur with the back of his finger, looking for any other signs of injury.

"Clean as a whistle!" he announces happily.

Like a newborn kitten or puppy, the baby rabbit's eyes are still closed. Squirming in the old man's hand, the little guy kicks and twists from side to side.

"Oh, ticklish, huh? Yessir, takes a lickin' and he's still kickin'!" laughs the old man. "You're a dandy, alright. Sure, just like your mama and grandma."

When the little rabbit continues to squeal, the old man strokes its fur slowly with his finger and reassures him, "Everything's okay. Sure, you're safe now. You're just a little frightened after all you've been through, that's all."

"Okay, now let's get you home to your mama — she's gotta be worried sick about her baby boy."

When the little guy is carefully placed in the deep, soft, dark pocket of the old man's vest, he quickly calms down and all squealing and kicking stops. Supporting the pocket gently with his hand from below to keep his tiny passenger from being jostled, the old man walks back across the meadow with long, slow, easy strides toward the burrow where he's sure Little-Bitty Bun will be nervously waiting.

As he nears the ransacked burrow, the old man can see its lining of fur and grass strewn all about the ground in big fleecy clumps tossed here and there by the huge crow. Little-Bitty Bun is crouched low near the burrow's entrance and it's plain to see that she is very distressed. Huddled down close to the ground with her ears laid back flat, she's trembling all over, as if she were suffering from a severe chill.

When she hears the old man's approaching footsteps, Little-Bitty Bun looks up hopefully, her ears perked up for any encouraging sound. "Everything's all right," he assures her. "We got your baby back all safe and sound, thanks to that ol' fat robin."

Kneeling down beside the distraught mother, the old man gently lifts the little rabbit out of his coat pocket. "Here's your baby," he coos warmly as he cradles the little guy in both hands.

Coming out into the bright sunlight, the little rabbit begins to squeal and squirm again. At the sound of her baby, Little-Bitty Bun's ears perk forward and her eyes open very wide. She puts her front paws up on the old man's knee, leans forward and nervously stares down at the little ball of fur.

"See, Mama, he's just fine," says the old man, smiling down at the two of them. Little-Bitty Bun just can't believe her eyes so she sniffs the little guy all over, nose to bum. Just to be sure, she sniffs him again, then gently touches her soft velvety nose to his.

"Here we go, let's get ol' junior back snug with his brothers'n sisters," says the old man, carefully putting the little rabbit back into the burrow. As he starts to replace some of the stray clumps of fur and grass lining, Little-Bitty Bun paws gently but firmly at his hand to let him know that she will take over now.

"Okay, Mama, you do that better than I do," he concedes. "You tidy up things around here and I'll be back in a little while."

Before leaving, the old man reassures the nervous mother, "And, don't worry about that ol' crow any more. After the shellackin' that ol' fat robin and his buddies gave him, he won't be comin' around here anytime soon. No way!"

The old man returns to his yard and, while crossing from the stream up toward the porch, he sees Fatty arrive back from chasing off the crow. Silently gliding up to and alighting on the birdbath beneath the fan-shaped mulberry tree, Fatty looks tired but no worse for wear. His beak is wide open as he pants to catch his breath.

"There's the guy that saved the day!" announces the old man, loudly. "Fatty, you ol' soldier, you're a hero! Yessir, you're the man!" he proclaims, just beaming all over with pride and admiration.

As the old man loudly praises his bravery, Fatty stands tall and regal, his head held high, his orange breast plumage all puffed out. He tilts his head slightly from side to side, casting his gaze over all the other birds and small animals nearby to be sure that everyone is taking notice of his moment.

The old man pauses, then laughs, "Hey, would you look at that! Your feather, that ol' cowlicky one — its gone! It musta come loose when you creamed that ol' crow."

Fatty peeks rearward, approvingly, at the spot where the wayward feather had once protruded so awkwardly.

"'Course that ol' crow left quite a few more feathers out there on the meadow than you did. Yessir, you and your buddies plucked him pretty good," the old man chuckles.

Very pleased with himself, Fatty takes a long cool sip of water, wades belly-deep into the birdbath and begins to dip and splash lustily, sending out a sparkling spray of water all around him.

Watching Fatty enjoying himself in the cool water, the old man says, "Boy, that sure looks good. I think I could use just a little of that, myself."

He turns on the hose and, waiting until the water spurts icy-cold, takes a long drink. Then, removing his hat and glasses, he bends forward at the waist and runs the water over his face, head and the back of his neck. Dropping the hose and turning off the water, he rubs his hands briskly around and around over his face and pushes back his wet hair from his forehead.

"Phew! Ah, that's the ticket," declares the old man. "There's nothin' like a garden hose on a warm day to cool off a fella — that's a fact, for sure."

Wiping his wet hands on his shirt and retrieving his glasses and hat, the old man steps up onto the porch and plops down in his chair to catch his breath. He takes out his big blue bandanna and slowly begins to clean his glasses, then stops and just stares off, quietly, out across the meadow for a long moment.

The old man sighs, "Yessir, Fatty, you and your buddies were a real godsend, today. I don't know what we'da done without you."

He gives his glasses a final wipe with the bandana and slowly puts them on. "Thank you," he says, his voice trailing off in a thin, dry whisper.

The Lord is good to all men, and his tender
care rests upon all his creatures.

Psalm 145: 9.

efore returning to check on Little-Bitty Bun and her family, the old man rests a while and re-ties one of his shoelaces. After another quick sip of water from the hose, he puts a fresh cookie into his shirt pocket, pulls on his hat and starts off toward the little hill out in the meadow.

As he trudges along, the old man spots a tiny, stubby-tailed, black vole scurrying along its shady above-ground tunnel through the grass. Kneeling down and leaning forward for a closer look, he gently parts the grass canopy over the inch-wide bare path trod by the little guy on his many repetitious foraging runs. But little Mr. Vole is much too occupied with his work to stop for even a brief chat, so the old man carefully closes the grass over the tunnel and continues on his way.

Arriving at the disheveled burrow, the old man sits down on the ground near Little-Bitty Bun. She's still very upset and has done nothing to repair the burrow while he was gone.

The old man gives her a small piece of cookie and talks to her in a soothing, reassuring tone while she eats. Soon, she appears much calmer and, after finishing with her cookie, she begins to lightly groom herself.

"I know you've got things to do, so I'll go away and let you get started," he tells her. "Everything's gonna be fine, now."

As the old man gets up, one of the baby rabbits crawls out of the burrow and totters blindly toward him. Without a moment's hesitation, Little-Bitty Bun turns her back to the burrow and, with a firm but gentle motherly nudge with a hind foot, sends the little guy rolling back in.

"Little bunny, corner pocket," chuckles the old man as he walks away. "Yessir, everything's gonna be just fine."

Hiking back across the meadow and recalling the afternoon's events, the old man's thoughts are interrupted by several loud, sharp, piercing chirps from the little woods off to his right.

"Hey, you chip-monkey," calls out the old man toward the sound. "It's okay, it's just me."

Walking toward the chirping, the old man comes to a small pile of dead tree limbs and brush heaped up in the tall grass at the edge of the woods. Close by, a tall catalpa or Indian bean tree is just coming into bloom with big heavy clusters of snowy white blossoms. Another chipmunk friend, named Thoreau, lives in these woods, in a burrow deep beneath the big roots of the catalpa tree. The old man has nicknamed this chipmunk "Speedy," because he's an exceptionally fast runner.

"Hey, Speedy, is that you?" calls out the old man. "It's just me."

In a moment, a chipmunk's head pops up among the dead limbs near the top of the brush pile. He peeks at the old man, then comes out and sits up on a large limb. Rubbing his paws rapidly over his head, from back to front, he fluffs his fur and combs out bits of grass and shreds of tree bark.

The old man begins rolling a peanut back and forth between his fingers, making a crackling sound with the broken shell. "Well, you comin,' Speedy?" he asks.

Thoreau disappears back into the heap of dead branches and quickly emerges on a slender limb protruding far out from the middle of the pile. As he moves further out on the limb toward the old man, the limb bends down under his weight. The further he goes, the lower it bends. When his "elevator" reaches the ground, Thoreau hops off and the limb springs back to its original position.

Weaving his way through the tall grass toward the old man, Thoreau hesitates for just a moment, then comes ahead.

"Sure, its just me, Speedy," says the old man as he kneels down and holds out three double-nutters in his fingers.

"How're you doin', you ol' chip-monkey?" he asks as Thoreau begins to stow the first peanut in his cheeks. The old man puts down the two remaining peanuts and takes out a handful more from his trousers pocket.

"I know you can't come up to the house today 'cause the creek's runnin' too full for a little chip-monkey to cross," he tells Thoreau. "So, I'm gonna leave a stash over here for you." Putting down the peanuts and bending grass over them for concealment, the old man tries to hide the pile from any prying eyes that might be watching.

"Now, keep this under your hat, Speedy," he advises, tapping the side of his nose with one finger. "If those fuzzytails or blue jays find out they'll steal'em for sure." Then, getting up and turning to leave, the old man adds, "I'll see you up at the house, tomorrow, when the creek's not runnin' so high."

Arriving back at his porch, the old man tosses down his hat, takes off his glasses and wipes his brow on his shirt sleeve. It's still more than an hour till dusk, but the sun has fallen behind the tallest trees in the little woods beyond the meadow and long shadows are slowly creeping across the yard toward the house.

"Looks like we're runnin' outta daylight," he complains. "Those pole beans'll just hafta wait till tomorrow. I guess it's best they soak overnight before plantin', anyway."

The old man brings out a cup of coffee, some cookies and his newspaper to the porch. Sitting down, he opens his paper across his lap and picks up his coffee cup in both hands. As he slowly sips his coffee, he stares out over the rim of the cup toward the meadow and Little-Bitty Bun's burrow. After a moment of scanning, he spots her near the edge of the tall grass, over by the small woods.

Little Bitty Bun carefully looks all around. In her mouth she has a large bunch of dried grass. Suddenly, she bounds high over the tall grass and weeds, in toward the tree line of the woods — then again, and again. With each jump, her ears are laid back flat and her scut, or tail, is turned white-fluffy-side down decreasing the chances of her being seen. Now, she's about ten feet back into the tall weeds and grass, near the brush pile where the old man had earlier visited with Thoreau. After a few more minutes, Little-Bitty Bun comes bounding high back out of the tall grass into the meadow. Now, her mouth is empty.

The old man puts down his coffee cup, leans forward and watches. About five minutes later, with a new mouthful of grass, Little-Bitty Bun repeats the process. Realizing that she's preparing a new home for her family, probably far under the brush pile, the old man mumbles to himself, "There's a smart girl. No ol' crow'll be gettin' after your babies, now."

Soon, perhaps after dark, Little-Bitty Bun will carry her babies in her mouth, one at a time, from the old burrow to their new home. On each trip, she will be careful to leap high over the tall grass and weeds that surround the brush pile, so as not to leave a telltale path of trod-down grass, or a scent trail, that could lead a predator to her new burrow. As a young mother, Little-Bitty Bun still has important lessons to learn, but she's a smart girl and is learning fast.

Go ask the cattle, ask the birds of the air to inform you, or tell the creatures that crawl to teach you, and the fishes of the sea to give you instruction. Who cannot learn from all these that the Lord's own hand has done this?

Job 12: 7-9.

s the old man leisurely enjoys his newspaper and coffee on his porch, the day quickly grows older. Out beyond the little woods, the sun is silently sliding below the horizon. The once dazzling transparent light of mid-day has mellowed and been broken by the lengthening shadows into random shafts of soft luminous yellow that make everything they touch appear to glow. The greens of the lawn, trees and gardens glimmer with an almost neon-like luster and, here and there, as swirling airborne congregations of tiny cellophane-winged insects drift slowly from shadow into light, they are transformed into bright shimmerimg puffs of gold dust.

Putting down his newspaper and coffee cup, the old man stands and slowly stretches his arms wide as he looks out over his yard and gardens. Up among the tree branches, the tiny chickadees' cheerful chorus of sundown chatter is counterpointed by the eerie calls of the catbirds and the robins' shrill protests against the coming darkness.

Old Mrs. Bun leisurely grazes on the lawn out by the big garden, looking up expectantly toward the porch between nibbles. Behind her, up on the long mounded-up asparagus plot, a few small dark bunny-shaped silhouettes show behind the backlighted gossamer-like veil of young green asparagus fronds.

"It's gettin' late," the old man announces. "Any little bunnies thinkin' about that ol' bedtime cookie?"

The old man takes a few raisin oatmeal cookies from his plate and stuffs his shirt pockets with peanuts. He gets up from his chair and walks out toward the rabbits. "Cookie time," he calls out. "Any cookie customers, tonight?"

Sitting down on the grass near the north end of the asparagus plot and with his back to the little stream, the old man starts to break up cookies into halves for adults and quarters for the smaller rabbits. Old Mrs. Bun comes right up for her cookie and, crouching down in the grass beside him, slowly savors each bite, her eyelids drifting halfway shut in peaceful bliss.

Two little rabbits peek from behind the asparagus fronds, then hop out to the oak ground rail that frames and shores up the plot's foot-high mound of earth and compost. "There's that Teeny Bun and Tiny Bun," notes the old man cheerily. "Those little sleepyheads missed their cookies this mornin' — they must be so-o-o hungry."

His two newest rabbit friends, they haven't yet mustered the courage to take their cookies from his hand. The pair inch toward the old man but stop just beyond his reach.

Meanwhile, Bittiest Bun scampers up from the far end of the asparagus plot, passing the two somewhat smaller rabbits, and stretches forward to receive her piece of cookie. Witnessing her trust and her reward, Teeny Bun and Tiny Bun creep a bit closer, but then hesitate and back away again.

"Close enough for this time," says the old man warmly as he gently tosses their cookies to them. "Maybe tomorrow, we'll get to know each other better."

Not to be left out, Itchy Bob and Shelley, dash across the lawn and hop up onto the old man's boots. The two smallest rabbits stare at the chipmunks with fascination as they load peanuts into their cheeks and dash back across the grass toward the house.

"Yeah, those little chip-monkeys are somethin' to see, aren't they?" the old man remarks. "You'll get used to 'em — sure, they're regulars around here. They're my buddies, too."

But now, having heard the old man's call for cookie customers and knowing this evening routine, several squirrels are converging on him and his rabbit friends. Some are striding boldly across the lawn. Others take routes through the canopy of the treetops, crossing from one tree to another, eventually reaching and descending the trunk of the big ash tree.

"Okay, all you fuzzytails, here you go," says the old man as he tosses out peanuts to them in rapid-fire succession. "Hurry up now, its getting late."

As the squirrels dash about madly after the flying peanuts, two or more often chase the same one, leading to collisions of bodies and egos. Some of these head-ons produce squabbling and testy chases, but most result in the startled colliders leaping high and away from each other, often with the loss of the peanut to both. The old man continues throwing out peanuts until every squirrel finds one and retreats high up the trunk of a tree or back across the lawn toward a neighboring yard.

As the last squirrel withdraws, a large rabbit leaps across the stream, landing almost in the old man's lap. "Here's that Little Bun," he announces. "Well, what's kept you so long?

You wouldn't wantta miss out on that ol' bedtime cookie, would you?"

Little Bun stands up high on his hind legs, receives his cookie and bites off a big mouthful, letting the rest of it fall to the grass in front of him. Then he crouches down to eat.

As Little Bun happily chews away, Bittiest Bun approaches him slowly and, assuming a very low submissive posture with her ears laid back flat, she shyly pushes her tiny nose low across the grass tops toward her uncle's nose.

Interrupting his meal for a moment, Little Bun also assumes a low, passive, ears-down stance and slowly stretches toward his tiny niece until their noses meet. After a few brief sniffs by each, Little Bun pulls away and resumes eating his cookie.

Bittiest Bun turns and hops up into the asparagus plot where the other two little rabbits are playing. She joins them in a game of chase beneath the fronds, all dashing around the long mound, in and out among the tall stalks, jumping up and kicking out gleefully with hind feet at every meeting.

Looking over at Little Bun as he sits up and wipes cookie crumbs from his mouth with his paws, the old man remarks, "Well, I guess every-bunny's all cookied up, now — all except for that Little-Bitty Bun."

At the mention of Little-Bitty Bun's name, Old Mrs. Bun stops nibbling clover and looks up at the old man, then stares out across the meadow toward the little hill.

"She's a little too busy tonight with her babies and her new burrow, but she'll be here in the mornin' for that ol' breakfast cookie," reassures the old man.

"Sweet, sweet," squeaks a tiny voice from up in the ash tree.

"Oops, can't forget about my other little buddies. Here we go, here come those ol' peanuts, guys," says the old man, looking up and smiling at the titmouse.

"Tsee-tsee-tsee," the chickadee chimes in.

"I've got some for you too," the old man assures him. "I'm comin', guys. I'm comin'."

As the old man nears the big bird feeder, cracking and shelling peanuts as he walks, several more birds gather overhead in the ash tree's branches.

"Lotsa peanut customers, tonight," notes the old man, cheerily. "There's ol' Mr. Cardinal and Missy Cardinal, and even Mr. and Mrs. Finch. And there's that little downy woodpecker and that ol' red-bellied woodpecker, too — howya doin' tonight, Red?"

After scattering several peanut halves in the feeder tray, the old man steps back and watches approvingly as each bird comes down, picks out a tasty morsel and flies off. "That's the stuff, guys," he urges. "Everybody belly up."

"Ding-dong, ding-dong," sounds a blue jay from over in the little fan-shaped mulberry tree.

"Who's that, the Avon lady?" asks the old man, sarcastically. Then, looking around, "Oh, its you, Jasper. Whatta you want, as if I couldn't guess?"

"Wheedle, wheedle, wheedle," pleads the jay.

"You know, you weren't a very good boy, today," the old man reminds him. "And after you promised to try."

"Wheedle, wheedle, wheedle," the jay insists.

"Okay, okay," says the old man, tossing out a peanut. "I guess we can give you another chance. But now, let's try just a little bit harder tomorrow, huh?"

The jay makes no reply, but only dives to the peanut, snatches it up and darts off low across the neighbor's yard.

"We may have a lost cause with that one," mutters the old man, sadly shaking his head.

"Dee-dee," observes the chickadee.

"Indeed, indeed," agrees the old man as he heads back over to the asparagus plot.

Re-joining the rabbits, the old man sits down on the ground beside Old Mrs. Bun and leans back against a corner post of the garden fence. Soon, the flickering of fireflies comes alive throughout the yard, all across the meadow and in the little woods. Overhead, against the dim blue sky and hazy pink-edged clouds, two small brown bats appear. Fluttering high enough to skirt the top of the apple tree, they drop down over the raspberry trellises before turning back low along the little stream and asparagus plot into the deepening darkness beneath the big ash tree. Around and around they go, silently scooping up mosquitoes and gnats, traversing the yard and gardens again and again.

"Well guys, the night shift's checked in," notes the old man reluctantly as he gets up to his knees. "Yessir, those ol' flip-floppy bats are gettin' after those skeeters and those ol' lightnin' bugs are turnin' on their night-lights for us. That means its little bunny bedtime — sure, time to say, 'Night-night.'"

On his feet, the old man slowly stretches rearward, then turns and walks toward the house, "Well, g'night, Bun, you ol' sweetie pie. G'night guys. Sweet dreams, everybody."

At the porch, he turns back and calls out, "Snuggle up, all you bunnies — chip-monkeys, too. Tomorrow, we've gotta get those pole beans planted, for sure. Everybody sleep tight and I'll see you in the mornin' for that ol' breakfast cookie."

The old man picks up his empty coffee cup and newspaper from the little table, opens the back door and steps in. Soon, the dim glow of a light comes on far back in the house, then he reappears in the doorway. For a long quiet moment he stands there, motionless, only a faint silhouette in the darkness.

"Night-night, sleep tight," he whispers, and the door slowly closes ... until tomorrow.

 End